Old Mother Goose
and Other Nursery Rhymes

Illustrated by
Alice and Martin Provensen

A Golden Book · New York

Western Publishing Company, Inc., Racine, Wisconsin 53404

Old Mother Goose

Old Mother Goose,
When she wanted to wander,
Would ride through the air
On a very fine gander.

On Christmas Eve

On Christmas Eve I turned the spit;
I burnt my fingers, I feel it yet;
The cock sparrow flew over the table,
The pot began to play with the ladle;
The ladle stood up like an angry man
And vowed he'd fight the frying pan;
The frying pan behind the door
Said he never saw the like before;
And the kitchen clock I was going to wind
Said he never saw the like behind.

Sing Song!
Merry Go Round

Sing song! Merry go round,
Here we go up to the moon, O!
Little Johnny a penny has found,
And so we'll sing a tune, O!

One, Two, Buckle My Shoe

One, two, buckle my shoe;
Three, four, shut the door;
Five, six, pick up sticks;
Seven, eight, lay them straight;
Nine, ten, a good fat hen;
Eleven, twelve, dig and delve;
Thirteen, fourteen, maids are courting;
Fifteen, sixteen, maids in the kitchen;
Seventeen, eighteen, maids are waiting;
Nineteen, twenty, my platter's empty.

Hickory, Dickory

Hickory, dickory, dock!
The mouse ran up the clock;
The clock struck one,
And down he run,
Hickory, dickory, dock.

Yet Didn't You See

Yet didn't you see, yet didn't you see,
What naughty tricks they put upon me?
They broke my pitcher
And spilt my water
And buffed my mother
And chid my daughter
And kissed my sister instead of me.

The Little Mice

This little mousie peeped within;
This little mousie walked right in!
This little mousie came to play;
This little mousie ran away!
This little mousie cried, "Dear me!
Dinner is done and it's time for tea!"

The Muffin Man

O do you know the muffin man,
The muffin man, the muffin man,
O do you know the muffin man
That lives in Drury Lane?

To Market, To Market

To market, to market, to buy a fat pig,
Home again, home again, jiggety-jig.

To market, to market, to buy a fat hog,
Home again, home again, jiggety-jog.

To market, to market, to buy a plum bun,
Home again, home again, market is done.

Two Gray Kits

Two gray kits and the gray kits' mother
All went over the bridge together.
The bridge broke down, they all fell in;
"May the rats go with you," says Tom Bolin.

Ding, Dong, Bell!

Ding, dong, bell!
Pussy's in the well!
Who put her in?
Little Johnny Green.
Who pulled her out?
Little Johnny Stout.

What a naughty boy was that
To try to drown poor pussycat,
Which never did him any harm,
But killed the mice in his father's barn!

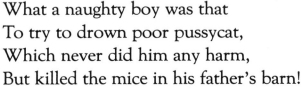

The Cats of Kilkenny

There were once two cats of Kilkenny,
Each thought there was one cat too many;
So they fought and they fit,
And they scratched and they bit,
Till, excepting their nails
And the tips of their tails,
Instead of two cats, there weren't any.

The Cats' Serenade

The cats went out to serenade
And on a banjo sweetly played;
And summer nights they climbed a tree
And sang, "My love, oh, come to me!"

Three Blind Mice

Three blind mice! Three blind mice!
See how they run! See how they run!
They all ran after the farmer's wife;
She cut off their tails with a carving knife.
Did you ever see such a sight in your life
As three blind mice?

The News of the Day

"What is the news of the day,
Good neighbor, I pray?"
"They say a balloon
Is gone up to the moon!"

A Farmer Went Trotting

A farmer went trotting upon his gray mare,
Bumpety, bumpety, bump!
With his daughter behind him, so rosy and fair,
Lumpety, lumpety, lump!

A raven cried croak! And they all tumbled down,
Bumpety, bumpety, bump!
The mare broke her knees and the farmer his crown,
Lumpety, lumpety, lump!

The mischievous raven flew laughing away,
Bumpety, bumpety, bump!
And vowed he would serve them the same the next day,
Lumpety, lumpety, lump!

Three Young Rats

Three young rats with black felt hats,
Three young ducks with new straw flats,
Three young dogs with curling tails,
Three young cats with demi-veils,
Went out to walk with two young pigs,
In satin vests and sorrel wigs;
But suddenly it chanced to rain,
And so they all went home again.

The Schoolroom Clock

There's a neat little clock—
In the schoolroom it stands—
And it points to the time
With its two little hands.
And may we, like the clock,
Keep a face clean and bright,
With hands ever ready
To do what is right.

Ride Away, Ride

Ride away, ride away,
Johnny shall ride,
And he shall have pussycat
Tied to one side;
And he shall have little dog
Tied to the other,
And Johnny shall ride
To see his grandmother.

Twinkle, Twinkle, Little Star

Twinkle, twinkle, little star,
How I wonder what you are!
Up above the world so high,
Like a diamond in the sky.

When the blazing sun is gone,
When he nothing shines upon,
Then you show your little light,
Twinkle, twinkle, all the night.

A Family Drive

Old Bob, young Bob,
Little Bob and big,
Molly Bob and Polly Bob,
And Polly Bobby's pig,
All went for a drive one day
And, strange as it may seem,
They drove six miles and back again
And never hurt the team.

Dance to Your Daddie

Dance to your daddie,
My bonnie laddie;
Dance to your daddie,
My bonnie lamb;
You shall have a fishy,
On a little dishy;
You shall have a fishy,
When the boat comes home.

The North Wind

The north wind doth blow,
And we shall have snow,
And what will the robin do then,
    Poor thing?

He'll sit in the barn
And keep himself warm,
And hide his head under his wing,
    Poor thing!

I Had a Little Nut Tree

I had a little nut tree; nothing would it bear
But a silver nutmeg and a golden pear.
The king of Spain's daughter came to visit me,
And all was because of my little nut tree.
I skipped over water, I danced over sea,
And all the birds in the air couldn't catch me.

Margaret Wrote
a Letter

Margaret wrote a letter,
Sealed it with her finger,
Threw it in the dam
For the dusty miller.

Dusty was his coat,
Dusty was the siller,
Dusty was the kiss
I'd from the dusty miller.

London Bridge

London Bridge is falling down,
Falling down, falling down,
London Bridge is falling down,
My fair lady.

Build it up with iron bars,
Iron bars, iron bars,
Build it up with iron bars,
My fair lady.

Iron bars will bend and break,
Bend and break, bend and break,
Iron bars will bend and break,
My fair lady.

Where Are You Going, My Pretty Maid?

"Where are you going, my pretty maid?"
"I'm going a-milking, sir," she said.
"May I go with you, my pretty maid?"
"You're kindly welcome, sir," she said.

Ifs and Ands

If "ifs" and "ands"
Were pots and pans,
There'd be no need for tinkers' hands.

Tommy Tonsey

Tommy Tonsey's come from France,
Where he learned the latest dance;
He has brought a scarlet dog,
And now the town is all agog.

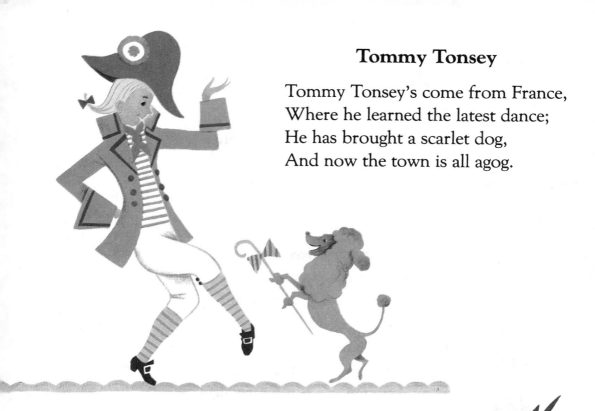

Tweedle-dum and Tweedle-dee

Tweedle-dum and Tweedle-dee
Resolved to have a battle,
For Tweedle-dum said Tweedle-dee
Had spoiled his nice new rattle.

Just then flew by a monstrous crow
As big as a tar-barrel,
Which frightened both the heroes so,
They quite forgot their quarrel.

Dance, Thumbkin, Dance

Dance, Thumbkin, dance;
Dance, ye merrymen, everyone.
For Thumbkin, he can dance alone,
Thumbkin, he can dance alone.

Dance, Foreman, dance;
Dance, ye merrymen, everyone.
For Foreman, he can dance alone,
Foreman, he can dance alone.

Dance, Longman, dance;
Dance, ye merrymen, everyone.
For Longman, he can dance alone,
Longman, he can dance alone.

Dance, Ringman, dance;
Dance, ye merrymen, everyone.
But Ringman cannot dance alone,
Ringman cannot dance alone.

Dance, Littleman, dance;
Dance, ye merrymen, everyone.
For Littleman, he can dance alone,
Littleman, he can dance alone.

Hark! Hark!

Hark! Hark! The dogs do bark,
Beggars are coming to town;
Some in rags and some in tags,
And some in velvet gowns.

Humpty Dumpty

Humpty Dumpty sat on a wall,
Humpty Dumpty had a great fall;
All the king's horses and all the king's men
Couldn't put Humpty Dumpty together again.

I Saw a Ship A-Sailing

I saw a ship a-sailing,
A-sailing on the sea;
And, oh! It was all laden
With pretty things for thee!

There were comfits in the cabin,
And apples in the hold;
The sails were made of silk,
And the masts were made of gold.

The four-and-twenty sailors
That stood between the deck
Were four-and-twenty white mice
With chains about their necks.

The captain was a duck,
With a packet on his back;
And when the ship began to move,
The captain said, "Quack! Quack!"

Three Little Kittens

Three little kittens, they lost their mittens,
And they began to cry,
"Oh, Mother dear, we sadly fear
   Our mittens we have lost!"

"What! Lost your mittens, you naughty kittens!
Then you shall have no pie."
"Meow, meow, meow!"

The three little kittens found their mittens,
And they began to cry,
"Oh, Mother dear, see here, see here,
   Our mittens we have found."

"What! Found your mittens, you good little kittens!
Then you shall have some pie."
"Purr, purr, purr."

Daffy-down-dilly

Daffy-down-dilly has come up to town
In a yellow petticoat and a green gown.

I Sing, I Sing

I sing, I sing,
From morn till night,
From cares I'm free,
And my heart is light.